An Aboriginal Story

How the kangaroos got their tails

Told by
George Mung Mung Lirrmiyarri

Compiled by
Pamela Lofts

SCHOLASTIC
SYDNEY AUCKLAND NEW YORK TORONTO LONDON

I'm going to tell you a story about how the kangaroos got their tails.

In the early days, in the Dreamtime,
there were two kangaroos who lived in this country.

One came from the hills,
the other from the plains.

The plains kangaroo was a big kangaroo
with long arms and long legs.

The hill kangaroo was a small kangaroo
with short arms and short legs.

One day the short-armed kangaroo was walking around
hunting for sugarbag (wild bush honey).

You can find sugarbag by watching the bees,
and following them to their hive where they make the honey.

He really liked sugarbag, that short-armed kangaroo,
so he kept on looking and looking
until he found some in a hole in a rock.

He reached just inside that hole and pulled out
a handful of sugarbag and ate it.

Mmmm. It was good tucker!

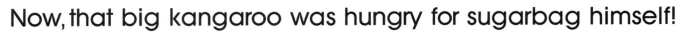
Now, that big kangaroo was hungry for sugarbag himself!

He sat down next to the short-armed kangaroo.
'Hey, what are you eating?' he said.
'I'm eating sugarbag,' said the short-armed kangaroo.
'You've got long arms, you can reach right down
and get some too!'

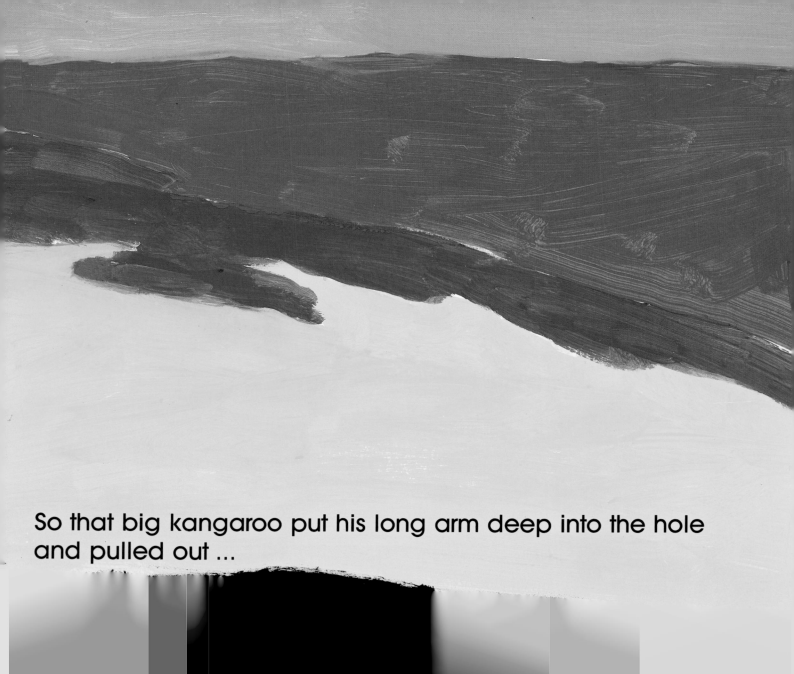

So that big kangaroo put his long arm deep into the hole
and pulled out ...

a handful of spiders!

Ugh!

'Try again,' said the short-armed kangaroo.
'Put your arm right down into the hole –
that's where the sugarbag is!'

So the big kangaroo put his hand into the hole again ...
but only pulled out more spiders.

The short-armed kangaroo kept reaching
just inside the hole ...
and pulling out more and more sugarbag.

Pretty soon he'd eaten it all himself.

The big kangaroo was wild!
That short-armed kangaroo had tricked him!
He went over to a white gum tree
and broke off a big stick.

The short-armed kangaroo thought he'd better get a stick too.
He went and broke one off a red bloodwood tree.

And then they started to fight.

They hit each other over the head with those sticks until the big kangaroo ran away.

Well, that short-armed kangaroo threw his stick and it stuck right into the big kangaroo.

That made the big kangaroo even more wild,
so he turned round and threw his stick.
It stuck right into the short-armed kangaroo.

Then they each hopped away back to their own country.
The big kangaroo went back to the low country
where the sugar-grass grows, and the short-armed kangaroo
hopped away up into the hills.

'I am a sugar-grass country man now,'
said that big, red, plains kangaroo.
'I will live here forever!'

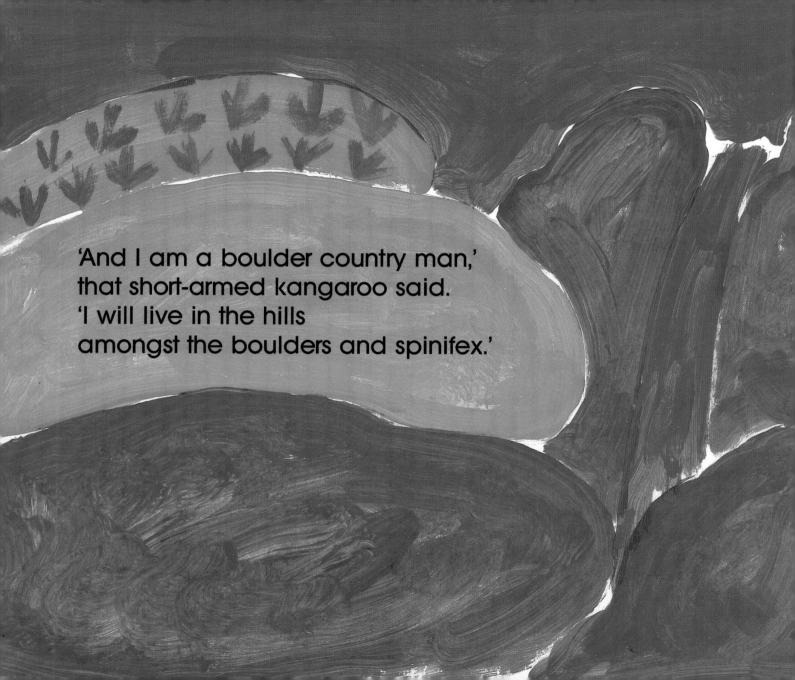

'And I am a boulder country man,'
that short-armed kangaroo said.
'I will live in the hills
amongst the boulders and spinifex.'

And they are still there today.
When you see them you will know how they got their tails.